Ming's Adventure on
China's Great Wall

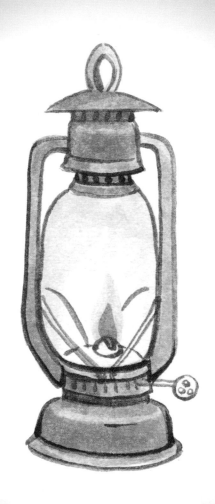

Copyright © 2015 by Shanghai Press and Publishing Development Company

This book is edited and designed by the Editorial Committee of *Cultural China* series

Story and Illustrations: Li Jian
Photograph: Zhai Dongfeng
Translation: Yijin Wert

Editorial Assistant: Logan Louis
Editor: Yang Xiaohe
Editorial Director: Zhang Yicong

Senior Consultants: Sun Yong, Wu Ying, Yang Xinci
Managing Director and Publisher: Wang Youbu

ISBN: 978-1-60220-987-9

Address any comments about *Ming's Adventure on China's Great Wall* to:

Better Link Press
99 Park Ave
New York, NY 10016
USA

or

Shanghai Press and Publishing Development Company
F 7 Donghu Road, Shanghai, China (200031)
Email: comments_betterlinkpress@hotmail.com

Printed in China by Shenzhen Donnelley Printing Co., Ltd.

1 3 5 7 9 10 8 6 4 2

长城

Ming's Adventure on
China's Great Wall

A Story in English and Chinese

by Li Jian

Translated by Yijin Wert

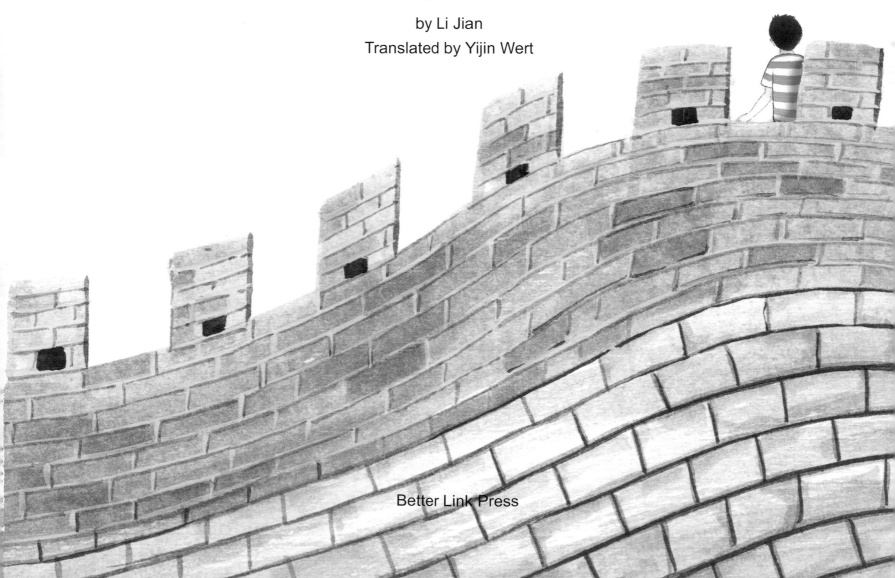

Better Link Press

Today, Ming was very excited because his father
decided to take him to the Great Wall.

今天，小明很高兴，爸爸要带他去登长城了！

Ming's father told him, "The Great Wall is over 6,300 kilometers long today. It was built, rebuilt, maintained and enhanced under many emperors for a period of over 2,000 years. Today, I am going to take you to the section called Badaling which is a part of the Great Wall lying just outside the city of Beijing."

In the far distance, the Badaling Great Wall looks like a gigantic dragon winding its way along the mountain ranges.

爸爸告诉他说:"今天,长城的长度超过 6300 公里。2000 多年的时间里,很多皇帝都曾修建、重建、维修、加固长城。今天我要带你去离北京不远的八达岭长城。"

远处,八达岭长城像一条巨龙匍匐在连绵起伏的山峰上。

Badaling Great Wall has a history of over 500 years. The castle-fortress at the entrance was magnificent.

八达岭长城有500多年历史了，入口处的关城好高大。

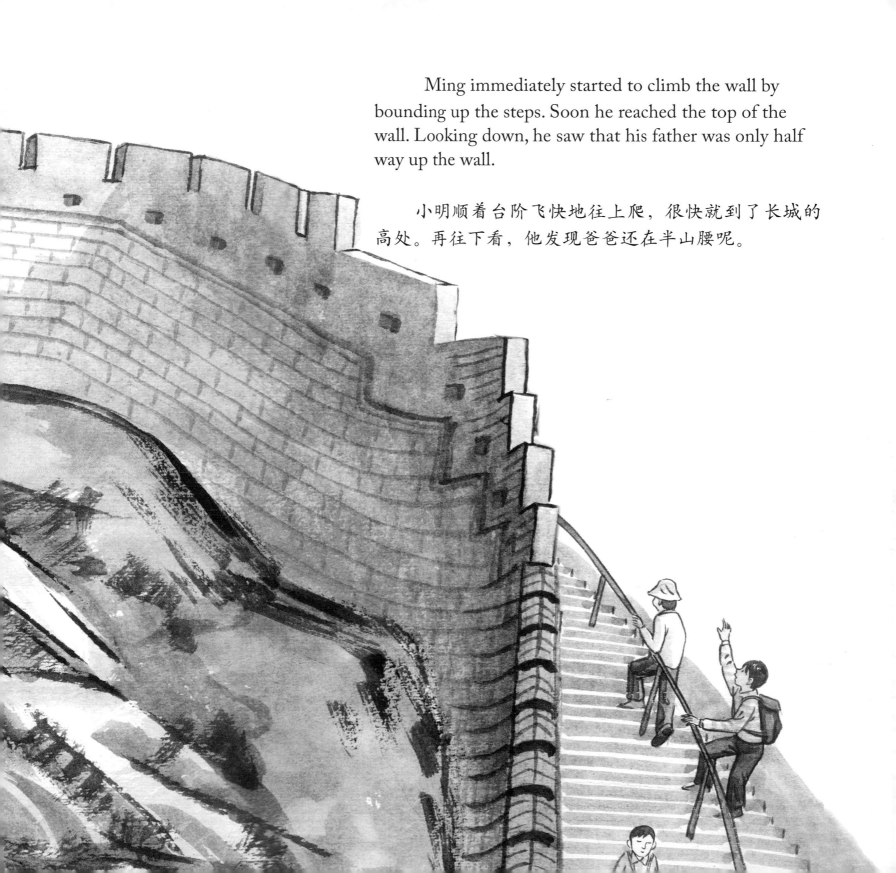

Ming immediately started to climb the wall by bounding up the steps. Soon he reached the top of the wall. Looking down, he saw that his father was only half way up the wall.

小明顺着台阶飞快地往上爬，很快就到了长城的高处。再往下看，他发现爸爸还在半山腰呢。

Ming was looking around as he walked along the wall. There, he had a birds-eye view of the beautiful scenery stretching out for miles.

Before he knew, it was already getting dark.

小明顺着城墙边走边看。居高临下，视野开阔，方圆几里内的美丽景象尽收眼底。

不知不觉间，天色渐渐暗了。

Suddenly, he saw some light in the distance. He walked towards the light, and there he saw a soldier in armor standing with a light in his hand.

突然，他看见前方有光亮。他向着光亮处走去，看见那里站着一个身穿铠甲的兵士，他的手里拿着一盏点亮的灯。

"My name is Ming, and I am here to visit the Great Wall with my father. Who are you? Why are you here?" Ming asked.

"I am the General who guards the Great Wall. I am ready to patrol around the area. Are you interested in coming along?" the General asked.

Ming gladly accepted the invitation. The General picked the wick.

"我叫小明，来这里跟爸爸游览长城。您是谁，为什么会在这里？"小明问。

"我是守护长城的将军，正要去各地巡逻，你想跟我去看看吗？"将军问。

小明高兴地接受了这个邀请。将军拨了一下灯芯。

As the light flickered, they were brought to a strange place. The General told Ming that they were at the State of Chu 2,600 years ago. The Great Wall being built there was in its infant stage.

灯光一闪，他们来到了一个陌生的地方。将军告诉小明说，这是2600多年前的楚国，正在修筑的城墙就是长城最早的雏形。

Then the General picked the wick again which brought him and Ming to the Qin Dynasty over 2,200 years ago. It happened that Qin Shihuang—the first emperor of China was on-site to inspect the Great Wall with his troops.

随后，将军又拨了一下灯芯，他和小明就来到了2200多年前的秦朝。恰逢秦始皇——中国的第一个皇帝率将士巡视长城。

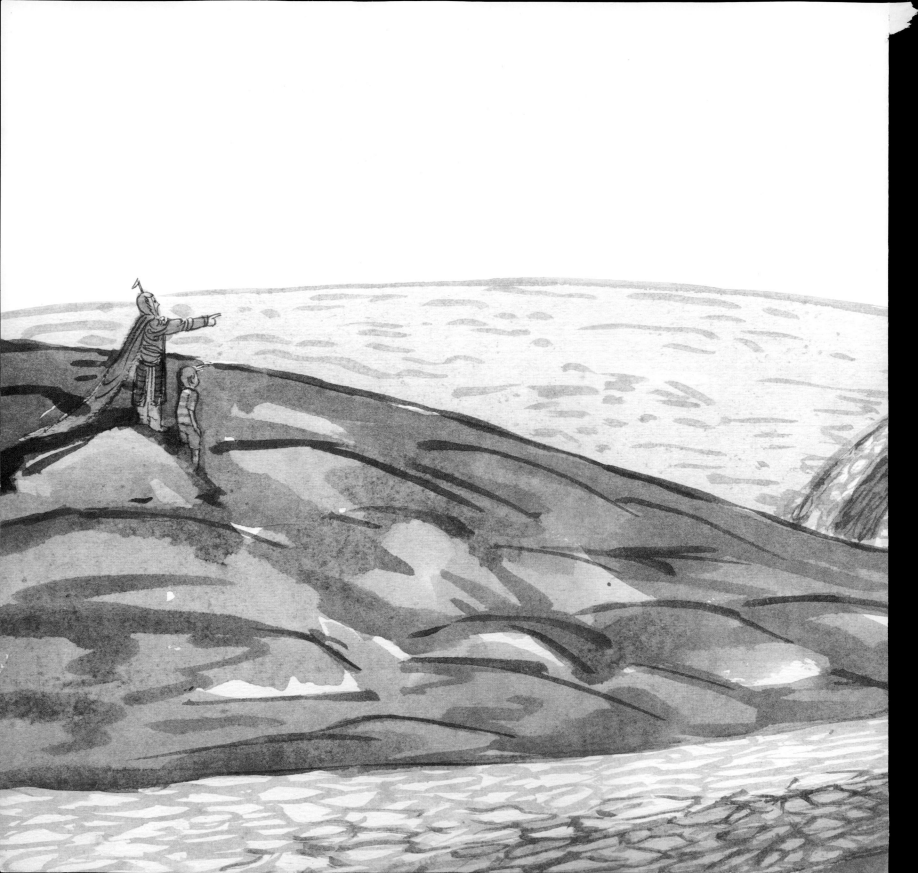

During the Han Dynasty over 2,000 years ago, the Great Wall was over 10,000 kilometer long.

2000年前中国汉朝的时候，长城已长达10000多公里。

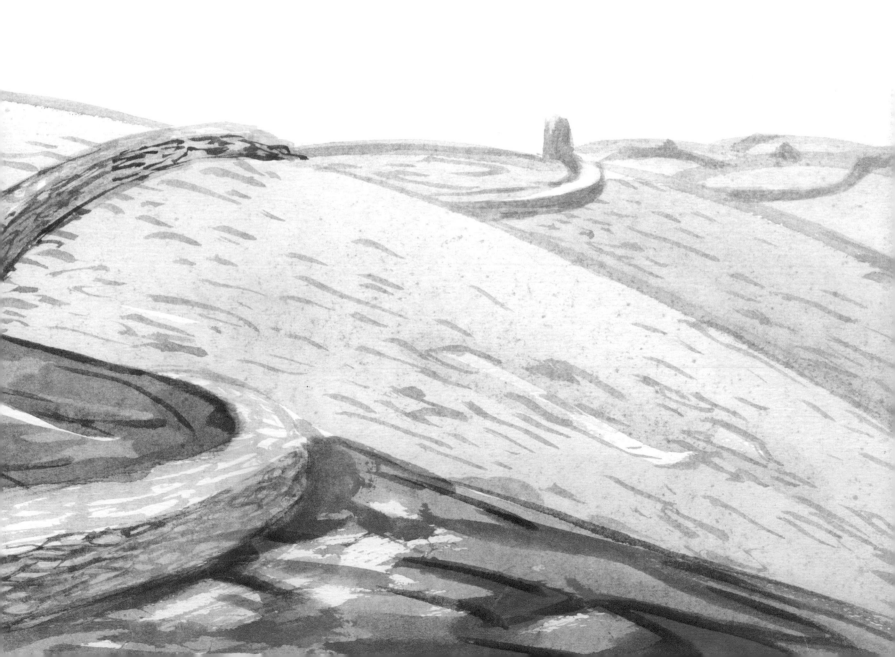

The wall, built in the Ming Dynasty about 600 years
ago, was best known for its well designed architecture.
It was extended immensely with more solid walls to
strengthen its defensive ability.

约600多年前的中国明朝则是长城修建工艺最高超
的时代。长城规模更巨大，更坚固。

The General took Ming to see the various unique sites
along the Great Wall …

将军带着小明去看各种各样奇特的长城⋯⋯

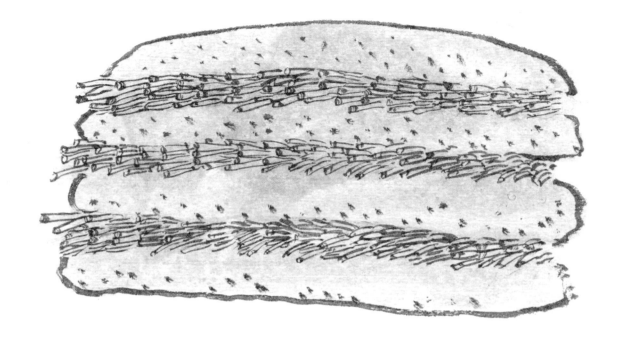

The foundation material of the Great Wall varied from dynasty to dynasty, from place to place. Some used earth, others used a mixture of gravel and straw, and others used the combination of bricks and stones …

不同朝代、不同地方建造长城的材质差异很大，有夯土的，有砾石和红柳混合的，有砖和石头混合的……

"This is an unbelievably large construction site," Ming said excitedly.

"Yes!" the General replied. "Based on the length of the Great Wall in the Ming Dynasty, it was estimated that the amount of stone and brickwork in its construction is more than enough to build a road that is 10 meters wide and 35 centimeters thick around the equator twice."

"这真是一个大工程！"小明兴奋地说。

"是呀！"将军说，"仅以明代长城估算，用去的砖石如果用来铺筑一条宽 10 米、厚 35 厘米的道路，可以绕地球赤道两周还多呢。"

The General explained, "During the war, the walls were used to defend against an invasion by the enemy. During peaceful time, the door of the castle-fortress to the wall was open to the public. Both the inside and the outside of the wall became a fair ground. Let's go and see."

将军解释说：“战争时，长城用来防御敌人进攻；和平时期，关城上的门则不再关闭，长城里外变成了集市。咱们也去逛逛吧！”

Just at that moment, the soldier at the watch tower shouted, "Enemies are coming! A troupe of soldiers are coming on their horses."

"Send the message immediately!" The General sent out the command calmly.

正在这个时候，瞭望台上的士兵大喊："敌人来了！他们骑着马，有几十个人！"

"快发出信息！"将军沉着下令。

Ming followed the General to the beacon tower and assisted the General to light the warning fire.

In a second, Ming saw the fire was lit on another beacon tower thousands of meters away. The fire was lit one after another. The message was passed from one beacon tower to another until it reached the Emperor. "It was so quick!" Ming was amazed.

小明跟着将军快步登上烽火台，帮助将军燃起了烽火。

不一会儿，小明看到数千米之外的另一个烽火台也燃起了烽火。一站接一站，消息在快速传递，直达皇宫。小明惊呼："太神速了！"

Suddenly, the General heard someone shouting.
"Someone is looking for you," the General said to Ming.
Then he quickly picked the wick again.

突然，将军听到有人在大喊。"有人在找你！"将
军对小明说。随后他飞快地拨了一下灯芯。

"Ming!" Ming saw his father waving to him anxiously.

As he turned around, he noticed that the General was gone and he was back at the Badaling Great Wall.

"小明！" 小明看到焦急的爸爸在向他招手。

一回头，小明发现将军不见了，自己已经回到了八达岭长城。

China's Great Wall in Photographs

The Great Wall of China is one of the seven greatest wonders in the world.

中国长城是世界七大奇迹之一。

The Capital View Tower (Wang Jing Lou) is so named because the Ming soldiers who manned it could see all the way to Beijing.

望京楼因明朝将士能从这里看到北京而得名。

In the early morning hours, it isn't unusual for people to find themselves as the only visitors to the wild but beautiful Jinshanling Wall.

清晨，人们常发现自己是荒僻而美丽的金山岭长城上唯一的游客。

Mist shrouds the slopes of the Jinshanling Mountain range, creating an ethereal setting for the Great Wall.

薄雾笼罩着金山岭山脉的山坡，为长城创造了一个空灵的意境。

The Jiu Yan Lou (Nine-Eyed Tower) in Beijing is equipped with a row of nine arrow ports on each of its four sides, making it the only watchtower with 36 ports.

北京九眼楼四边各有九个瞭望孔，是唯一一座有36个瞭望孔的敌楼。

Shanhaiguan Pass, situated northeast of Qinhuangdao of Hebei Province, was the most important fort at the eastern end of the Great Wall.

坐落在河北秦皇岛东北部的山海关是长城东端最重要的要塞。

In Shanxi Province, the core of a beacon tower is the centerpiece of a watermelon patch farmed by the locals.

在山西省，烽火台的遗址位于当地农民一片西瓜地的中心。

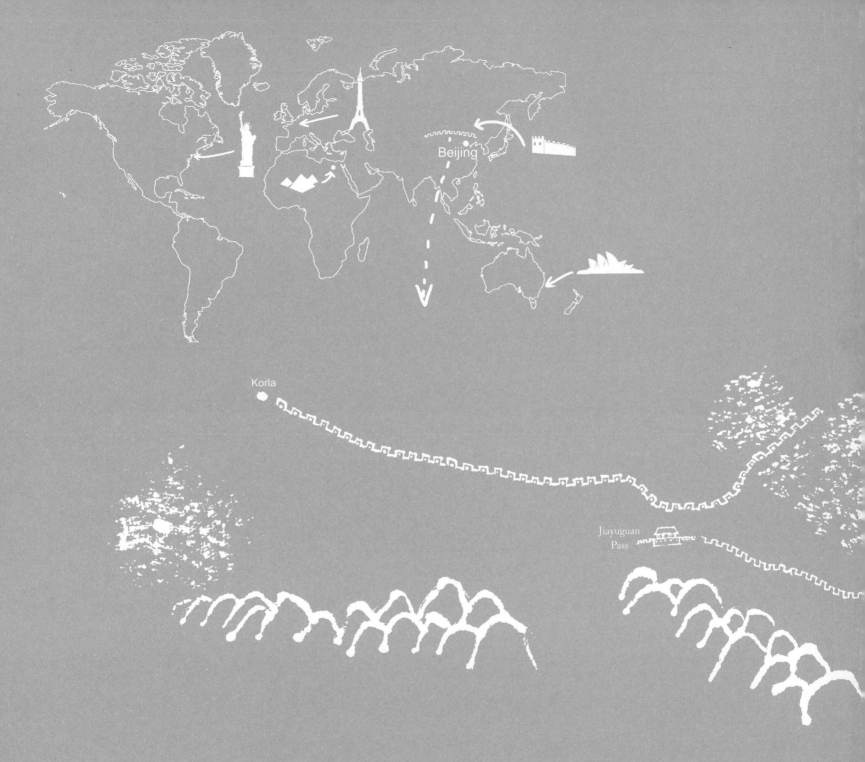

Beijing

Korla

Jiayuguan
Pass

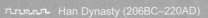